All the Wave

Written by
Tiana Woolridge

Illustrated by
Eleanor Jones

To my father, **Orlando Woolridge**, and his sister, **Vanessa Woolridge**:

Thank you for adding to the sum of human joy.

Ness loved the water.

She loved watching water fall from the sky into big puddles, puddles so big she could jump into with her big pink rain boots.

She loved scooping water into her hands during bath time and watching it drip slowly from her fingers.

She loved crawling up
onto the kitchen counter so her
mom could wash her hair in the sink,
and feeling water weigh down her thick curls.

Her big brother Orlando didn't love water as much as her. But they were best friends, so when she begged him to make cannonballs together in their pool, he always said: "**Yes!**"

Saturdays were her favorite, because that was the day everyone could go to the place where you could see the most water at once: **the beach!**

Her 7th birthday was coming up, and guess what: it was on a **Saturday**!
All of her best friends would be able to play in the water with her.

That morning, she woke up before the sun and ran to her brother's room, shouting in excitement: **"Today is my beach birthday party!"**

Once everyone finally made it to the beach, Ness ran straight to the ocean. There it was, sparkling and splashing playfully along the shore.

Her friends decided they should build a giant sandcastle for her birthday. Everyone grabbed their buckets and ran down to the water.

To get the best building sand, they waited until the waves pulled back into the ocean, scooped up as much wet sand as they could, and then ran back up to the beach before the waves returned.

Ness loved doing this. It felt like a game with the ocean! They all giggled and shrieked every time they tried to outrun the waves.

One time, she noticed that the sand around her feet was sliding backwards but the sand under her feet was still. Fascinated, she knelt to look closer, not noticing her friends running past her.

All of a sudden…

CRASH!

Ness was flat on her face and then up-side down and then right-side up, spinning out of control while being dragged backwards into the ocean.

She saw nothing but a dark, angry blue, and a loud whooshing sound pressed into her ears. Her gentle, sweet, bubbling water was now a **terrifying, swirling monster** trying to take her away from her friends, her family, and everything she knew and loved.

Ness couldn't figure out where she was, or what direction was up or down. As she began to give up hope that she would ever escape, she felt two strong hands grab her and pull her out of the darkness.

Coughing, blinking the sting of salt water from her eyes, Ness could barely recognize Orlando standing over her, much less the scared look on his face.

She burst into tears and jumped into his arms. Through her tears, she declared:

"I **HATE** the water! I'm never coming back here again!"

Orlando squeezed her tighter and said, "Ness, it's okay. Turn around and look."

Sniffling and refusing to let go of her brother, she turned her head slightly to peek at her monster. To her surprise, it looked calm and beautiful, just like when she first got to the beach.

"The ocean is still wonderful and amazing," Orlando said. "But it is much bigger and stronger than you, so you have to be careful. And know that no matter what happens, **I'll always be there for you.**"

Ness nodded and wiped the tears from her eyes. She looked up at her big brother, who was smiling down at her, and felt a wave of love and warmth fill her chest.

"Thanks, O," she said, giving him another big hug. "Now let's go finish this castle – I bet I can beat you back up there!"

They ran off up the beach to rejoin her friends, as the ocean continued its endless splashing up and down the shore.

The End